The Coach, the Shoes and the Football

By Katie Dale

Illustrated by Ellie Oshea

Chapter 1

"Have you finished mopping the kitchen floor yet?" Raj's stepfather, Terry, called from upstairs.

"Just finished!" Raj replied, wiping his brow. It had taken ages.

"Good," Terry replied. "Then take out the rubbish, do the washing up, and put your stepbrothers to bed. I'm having a bath."

Raj's heart sank.

It was bad enough having an awful stepdad,
but his stepbrothers were even worse.
Raj really missed his mum.

Luke and Damon were both jumping on
their beds.

“Bedtime!” Raj said.

“I'm not sleepy!” Luke cried.

“Me neither!” Damon laughed.

“Please stop bouncing and get into bed,” Raj begged.

“Only if you read me a story!” Luke cried, grabbing a book and knocking over his glass of water.

"Yeah, read him Cinderella!" agreed Damon. "While you're cleaning my trainers."

Raj narrowed his eyes. "Why should I clean your shoes?"

"Because if you don't, I'll keep bouncing and you'll get into trouble with Dad," Damon said, grinning.

"Fine," Raj sighed as he grabbed a cloth. "Why Cinderella?"

"Because it's like us!" Damon said,

grinning. "You're Cinder-Raj!"

Luke giggled and Raj gritted his teeth. He wished he was Cinderella, but he didn't have a fairy godmother - just a hairy godfather called Dan. And there was no such thing as a happy ending. Not for Raj, anyway.

"You look tired, Raj," his teacher, Miss Brooks, said the next day. "Bet you're looking forward to the summer holidays!"

Raj's heart sank. Six weeks with his horrible stepfamily? He couldn't think of anything worse.

"Are you going to sign up for football summer camp?" Miss Brooks asked, handing him a leaflet. "Six weeks of football training with top coach Peter Prince."

Raj's heart rose, then sank like a brick when he saw the price. "It's very expensive."

"They're holding tryouts on Saturday," Miss Brooks said. "The winner gets a free place."

Raj's eyes lit up. A free place playing football all summer? Spending six weeks away from his horrible stepfamily? It would be a dream come true! And it was his birthday on Saturday! Maybe it was a sign?

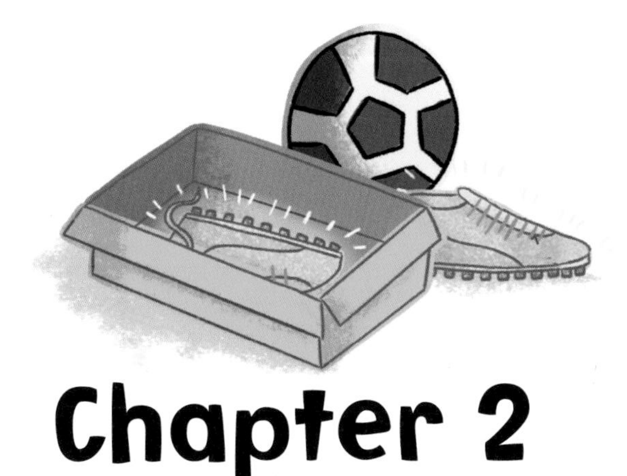

Chapter 2

Raj practised hard all week, but on the day of the tryouts he couldn't find his football boots anywhere.

"Looking for something?" Damon smirked.

"Did you take my boots?" Raj asked suspiciously.

"Maybe," Damon shrugged.

"Give them back!" Raj demanded.

"What's going on?" Terry cried, bursting into the room.

"Damon's hidden my football boots!" Raj cried.

"No I haven't!" Damon said.

"Liar!" Raj fumed.

"Don't call my son a liar!" Terry snapped. "Why do you need football boots, anyway?"

“Um... just to practise in the park,” Raj fibbed. He couldn't tell Terry about the summer camp until he definitely had a place. Terry would never let him go to the tryouts.

“Liar, liar, pants on fire!” Damon cried, handing his dad the football camp leaflet.

Raj's heart plummeted.

“Six weeks away?” Terry cried. “Who'd do all the chores?”

“Please, Terry!” Raj begged. “I'll do extra chores when I get back.”

“No way,” Terry said. “Besides, you're grounded for lying. Come on, Luke and Damon, let's go for ice-cream.”

“Hurray!” Luke cried.

“And Raj,” Terry added. “I want the garden weed-free by the time we get home.”

Raj sighed. It was so unfair! As he slumped outside, he devised a plan. He'd wait until his stepfamily left, then he'd sneak out to the tryouts.

But as he stepped into the shed to grab a spade, the door slammed shut behind him! Raj pushed it, but it was locked!

"That's for telling on me!" Damon hissed. "Anyway, I didn't lie. I stole your shoes, but Luke hid them!"

"Happy birthday, Cinder-Raj!" Luke called.

Raj slumped down on a paint pot. This was the worst birthday ever.

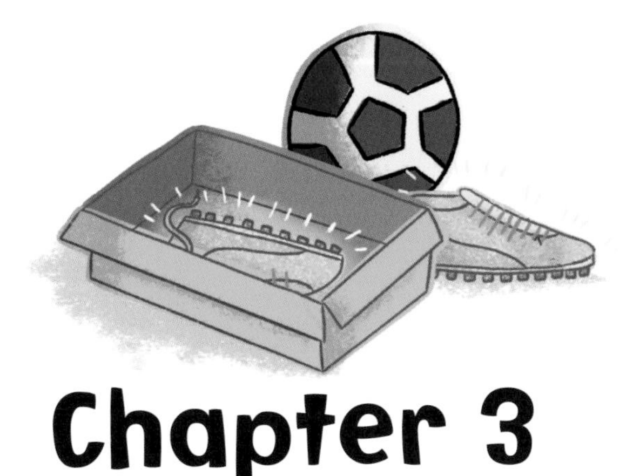

Chapter 3

Raj sat in the dusty shed for what seemed like hours, then suddenly he heard a clatter. He peered through the window and spotted his godfather, Dan, carrying a birthday present!

"Dan!" Raj called, rattling the door. "Help!"

"Raj!" Dan cried, hurriedly unlocking the door.

“I thought everyone was out, so I came round the back to leave your present somewhere safe. What happened? Who locked you in the shed?”

Raj told him.

“That's terrible!” Dan cried when Raj finished explaining. “I had no idea your stepfamily treated you so badly.”

“They're horrible!” Raj sighed. “But what can I do?”

“Well, for starters, you need go to the football tryouts!” Dan cried, jumping up. “Come on, I'll drive you!”

“I can't,” Raj said. “Luke hid my boots!”

“Then it's lucky I bought you a new pair for your birthday, isn't it?” Dan grinned, handing Raj his present.

“Thank you!” Raj cried, quickly opening the box. They were the strangest boots he'd ever seen!

“They're... sparkly!” Raj gasped.

“I couldn't afford a designer pair, sorry,” Dan said.

“No, these are great! Thank you!” Raj said quickly. “Let's go!”

Chapter 4

The tryouts were just starting when Raj and Dan arrived. Raj pulled on his new boots quickly. They were a perfect fit!

“Nice boots!” a boy smirked. Raj scowled.

Coach Prince led them in a warm-up, then the first test was a race. Raj sprinted as fast as he could.

His new boots were much lighter than his old ones, so he was faster than usual, and came second!

Next they did dribbling exercises. The ball seemed to stick to Raj's shoes like velcro as he dribbled easily around the cones.
He came first!

Finally everyone had to take penalties - against Coach Prince!

Nervously, one by one, everyone took their shots. One by one, Mr Prince saved all the penalties.

Raj was last. Raj stared at the ball, his palms sweating.

“Come on Raj!” Dan called. “You can do it!”

Raj swallowed hard, ran, aimed, and
KICKED!

WHOOSH!

The ball flew straight into the top right corner! And so did Raj's boot!

Mr Prince caught the shoe - but not the ball! Raj had scored!

“Hurray!” Dan yelled from the sidelines. “Go Raj!”

“Nice shoes,” Mr Prince grinned, returning Raj's boot. “And well done. You've worked really hard today and you've got real talent. I'd like to offer you a free place on my summer camp.”

“Really?” Raj couldn't believe his ears.

“Not so fast!” cried a voice. Raj turned to see his stepfather marching across the pitch.

Chapter 5

"Raj can't go to summer camp," Terry cried. "I forbid it."

“Yeah!” said Luke. “We need Cinder-Raj to do all the chores!”

Everyone gasped. Terry turned bright red.

“Raj won't be doing your chores anymore,” Dan said, stepping forward. “He's coming to live with me.”

Raj looked up in surprise.

“If he wants to,” Dan added quickly.

“Yes! Yes I do!” Raj said excitedly.

“You can't just take him from me,” Terry

argued. “I'm his stepfather.”

“And I'm his godfather,” Dan said, lowering his voice. “Unless you want me to tell everyone how you've been mistreating Raj and how I found him locked up in your shed, you'll let him come and live with me.”

Terry turned as purple as a beetroot. “Fine!” he snapped, turning on his heel and marching away.

Raj couldn't believe it. He was free of his horrible stepfamily! He was going to live with Dan! He was going to football camp!

It was like a dream come true. Maybe there was such a thing as a happy ending - after all, Raj had his very own hairy godfather, Coach Prince, new shoes and a ball!

“Are you okay, Raj?” Coach Prince asked.

Raj nodded. “This is the best birthday ever!”

He grinned. "I really do feel like Cinderella!"

"I hope not!" laughed Coach Prince. "She wouldn't make a very good footballer - she ran away from the ball!"

Raj laughed. That was one way they were **DEFINITELY** different!

Pink
Red
Yellow
Blue
Green
Orange
Turquoise
Purple
Gold
White

Book Bands for Guided Reading

The Institute of Education book banding system is a scale of colours that reflects the various levels of reading difficulty. The bands are assigned by taking into account the content, the language style, the layout and phonics. Word, phrase and sentence level work is also taken into consideration.

Maverick Early Readers are a bright, attractive range of books covering the pink to white bands. All of these books have been book banded for guided reading to the industry standard and edited by a leading educational consultant.

To view the whole Maverick Readers scheme, visit our website at
www.maverickearlyreaders.com

Or scan the QR code above to view our scheme instantly!